Modern Fairy Tales

Neil Stainthorpe

with illustrations by
Cornelia Kriechbaumer

Table of contents

Rumpelstiltskin

$$H_2O = Au?$$

1.   Rumpelstiltskin

Once there lived a young-ish king,
Who liked to drink and dance and sing,
Who, though his palace looked quite flash[1],
Was terminally[2] short of cash.

Imagine his surprise one day,
When Granny came to him to say,
"Hey King! I've heard the miller's daughter,
Spins pure gold just using water!"

The king said, "Granny, you misheard.
With you, "stone-deaf[3]" is not the word[4]!"
Granny said, "It's not a joke!
And, don't forget you're stony broke!"

Kingy, looking pained and wincing[5],
Answered, "This is not convincing!"
But just in case it might be true,
I know just what I'm going to do!"

Not a moment did he ponder,
Ran outside, jumped on his Honda.
To the river he did race,
Burst into the miller's place.

---

[1] flash – expensive-looking, trying to impress people
[2] terminally – (here) always
[3] stone-deaf – totally deaf
[4] ...is not the word – doesn't get close to describing sth. accurately
[5] wincing – with an expression of pain on your face

"Ok miller, I'm the king,
And I can order anything!
I've heard that you can help me out
With my latest cash flow drought[6].

Not you so much, as your fair daughter,
Who, I've heard, makes gold from water.
Bring her here and off we'll go.
A fortune made from H_2O!"

"O King, I hate to be a bore[7],
She can't do water, only straw!"
Before the week was two days old,
Some straw she had to spin to gold.

A spindle and a pile of straw,
She sat there staring at the door.
"Gold?" she thought, "I've no idea.
I don't know what I'm doing here!"

And so, she sat and cried until
The sun came up, her progress nil[8].
And just when she could cry no more,
She heard a knock upon the door.

In came a little man in green,
Looking neat and rather clean.
"Hello," he said, "This place is cold!
Then added, "Oops! Not much gold!

---

[6] drought – lack of water (cash flow drought - here – money)
[7] a bore – a boring person
[8] nil – nothing

The king is on a losing streak[9],
You're the third he's had this week.
I tell you what, you cry no more,
I'll use my magic on the straw!"

Before too long, if truth be told,
Was on the floor a pile of gold.
The king exclaimed, "It's been a blast![10]
But I want more of this, and fast!"

He gave them both his nicest smiles
And promptly ordered two more piles.
Didn't take them long to figure,
Both the piles were much, much, bigger.

---

[9] a losing streak – losing several times in a row
[10] it's been a blast! – It's been great fun!

The miller's daughter groaned and said,
"It's either this or bye-bye head!"
Looked over to the little man,
And said, "Ok! So, what's the plan?"

"An end that's neither fast nor tragic,
Needs an awful lot of magic.
I'll help you with the golden horde,
But how about a small reward?

That phone of yours looks rather fine,
I do the straw, the phone is mine!"
The deal was written down and then,
Both signed it with a ballpoint pen.

Two days on, the job was done,
The piles of straw completely spun.
The girl, however, loved her phone,
And so, she thought, "I'll start to moan."

 "I say!" she called across the cell.
"Life without my phone is hell!
Losing it would be a crime,
Without it, life's a waste of time!"

She paused and then she smiled so sweetly,
The old man's heart did melt completely.
He said, "Ok, we'll play a game.
You only have to guess my name!

Not easy!" said the man in green,
"Round here I'm not often seen."
She said, "I'll give it my best shot!"[11]
Then she asked how long she'd got.

---

[11] I'll give it my best shot – I'll try my best

"Well," he said, "The task's a bummer[12].
You can have until the summer.
Till outside the cows are mooing
And the contract needs renewing."

"Ok!" she said, "We've got a deal!"
And instantly began to feel,
"It's no big thing to win this bet,
I'll get the answer off the net.

As soon as I am on my own,
I'll log in on my mobile phone.
Type "green man" and "guessing game"
And in a flash, I'll have his name."

He lived remotely, his address
"The Middle of Nowhere," more or less.
No neighbours, telly, social media,
Instagram or Wikipedia.

But there is these days, you see,
No longer any privacy.
Although he didn't know or care,
His fame was spreading everywhere.

And since he never used the net,
He nearly always lost his bet.
Those guessing didn't waste their time,
They simply checked him out online.

Spring passed by and summer came,
The girl forgot about the game.
Till one day at ten to four,
The green man came in through the door.

---

[12] a bummer – something difficult or unpleasant

He bowed to her, said "Hi there, Queenie!
Where's my phone? Don't be a meanie!
The contract's done, it all looks fine.
At last! The royal phone is mine!"

"Hang about!" the new queen said,
"I think I'll say your name instead.
You see, the mobile is a hit,
I'm really quite attached to it.

Rumpy, dear, I really hate
To tell you you're not up to date.
You'll find you simply must acknowledge
That your name is common knowledge.[13]

---

[13] common knowledge – something that everybody knows

No need at all to track you down,
Find your cottage outside town,
Or eavesdrop[14] on your evening song
And guess which names are right or wrong."

Half an age the silence lasted.
Rumpy stood there, flabbergasted[15].
Then, slowly, he began to speak,
In a sort of high-pitched squeak.

"If everybody knows my name,
I'll lose the reason for my fame.
I won't be wanted any more,
My name is what I'm famous for.

You mean that everyone's found out?
I'm going to go and check this out.
I'll appear out of thin air,
And ask the people everywhere."

With a window-rattling "boom,"
He stamped his foot and left the room.
Vanished[16] with a flash of light,
And set off cursing in the night.

---

[14] eavesdrop – listen in on a conversation secretly
[15] flabbergasted – amazed, speechless.
[16] vanish – disappear

Hoody and the Wolf

2.   Hoody and the Wolf

There was a nice young girl called Hoody,
Well-behaved, a goody-goody.
As sweet as strawberry chewing gum.
She lived in town with her old mum.

People loved her, far and wide,
In town and in the countryside.
Her memory, though, when she got tired,
Left a bit to be desired.

One day mum said, "Granny's sick.
Her legs are swollen, two feet thick.
She's be home till she gets fitter.
I know, she told us all on Twitter.

She's low on food, not got enough.
So, Hoody, you can take some stuff!
I can't go, no time to spare,
I have to sell my Tupperware."

Mum gave her lots of good advice:
Important stuff she mentioned twice,
Knowing, though she would repeat it,
Hoody's brain would soon delete it.

"Ok, Hoody, take the wine
And cake to granny, she'll be fine.
You'll have to walk right through the wood,
So, listen here and listen good.

Just between your mum and you,
Here's some things you shouldn't do:
The wood is full of hidden dangers,
Don't leave the path or talk to strangers!"

But as we said, it was quite sad,
Her memory was really bad.
As soon as she was out the door,
She couldn't think straight any more.

Dressed in her red dressing gown[17],
She took the road straight into town.
She was hungry, bought some bread,
But fed it to the ducks instead.

She bought a paper, read the news.
Tried on jumpers, socks and shoes.
Skated round the skating park,
Prepared to stay till it was dark.

At roughly twenty-five past two,
She thought of what she had to do.
"I'm dumber than a sugar mouse!
I've got to go to granny's house!"

Her memories of mum's advice
Were somewhat more than imprecise.
No more than a thing or two -
No idea of what to do.

"Mum said, "Please don't use the path?"
Or did she say, "Don't have a bath?"
She also said "Don't talk to strangers!"
Or did she mention flower arrangers?

---

[17] dressing gown – piece of clothing people wear at home, like a long
coat, often made of flannel.

17

Was it "Hoody, come straight home!",
Or should I buy some shaving foam?
Well, I must say I don't care,
I love it in the open air!"

She got tired, and thought, "Oh crap!
I really wish I'd bought a map!"
She ate the cake and drank the wine,
And slowly started feeling fine.

She lay down in the flower bed.
"I'll have a snooze[18]," she quietly said.
"I need to get my thinking straight.
Granny's food'll have to wait."

She woke and thought, "I need a loo.
You see what red wine does to you!
And then I must be off to gran.
But which way? I'll ask that man!

He certainly looks rather scary,
Six foot tall and very hairy.
But mum said, "Please be kind to strangers,
Particularly flower arrangers!"

She looked across and shouted "Hi!
I'm waiting for a passer-by.
My poor old granny needs assistance
And I, the path of least resistance."

The wolf stood still and looked her way.
Saw young Hoody, thought "Hooray!
This seems to be a certain winner.
She doesn't know me – time for dinner!

---

[18] snooze – short sleep

Hello Hoody, hope you're fine!
What's in here? Lots of wine?
A thirsty girl, the weather's hot,
I can tell, you've drunk the lot!

A large plate with a cake for me –
At least - that's where it used to be.
It must have been so very big,
You ate the lot, you greedy pig!"

"Ah! You're the man who does the flowers!
You must have waited here for hours!"
The wolf said, "What? Eh? Oh, yeah, right!
I think about them day and night."

So, he thought, "I'll soon impress her,
Sound just like a flower professor!"
So, he started his narration
Of dubious[19] flower information.

"You want flowers, I'm your man!
I can name them all, I can!
There are flowers all around you.
My subject knowledge will astound[20] you!

Roses, tulips... er ... these are peas,
Daffodils, er ... cottage cheese.
This edelweiss is Pakistani!
Grab a bunch, we'll go to granny."

---

[19] dubious – not very accurate
[20] astound – amaze

Meanwhile Hoody's mum was scared.
"Gran's done it now!"[21] she then declared.
"I'm really seriously shocked.
She wrote she left the door unlocked!

She uses Twitter, not WhatsApp
Because she thinks WhatsApp is crap.
But now she's gone and lost her head
She wrote it on WhatsWolf instead!!"

The wolf thought, "Now, it's time to eat!
I'm almost dying on my feet.
It's time we went to granny's place,
To fill my tummy storage space."

Just as things were looking dire,[22]
They heard a screeching[23] motor tyre.
Approaching quickly, from afar,
A football-shaped, red motor car!

And in it sat an egg called Humpty.
(Proper name was Humpty Dumpty)
This Humpty egg was round and fat.
That's why his car was made like that.

He stopped the car, then, wobbling[24] slightly,
Introduced himself politely.
"Humpty Dumpty is the name.
I live nearby, enjoy great fame.

---

[21] She's done it now! – She's really made a big mistake
[22] dire – very bad
[23] screech – a loud, unpleasant noise, (here) a car braking very quickly
[24] wobble – rocking slightly from side to side

I feature in a nursery rhyme[25],
Children read it all the time.
I sometimes fall and crack my shell,
And then I feel a bit unwell.

I use glue to mend[26] the cracks.
I claim it all against my tax.
The car, as well, makes perfect sense,
A necessary job expense."

Humpty stated, quite exultant,[27]
"I'm a full-time wolf consultant.
You just tell me where they are,
I'll get them with my motor car!

That usually does it, failing that,
I sit on them and squash them flat.
Or I knock them on the head,
Then they're usually fairly dead."

"Hoody, dearest, can I help?"
The wolf began to quietly yelp.
Inwardly he gave a groan,
"This wolf consultant is well-known!"

"Well, I suppose it's bye-bye dinner.
My chances here are getting thinner.
He'll sit on me and then that's that.
There'll just be one fantastic "splat"!"

---

[25] nursery rhyme – rhyme for young children
[26] mend – repair
[27] exultant – very happy

The wolf revised the situation,
Opted for[28] a new location.
Without a glance to left or right,
Accelerated[29] out of sight.

Hoody shook her head, surprised,
"I don't think that I realised
That egg-based help is quite the best.
Humpty, I am most impressed!

I must tell mum, it's undeniable,[30]
Her advice is unreliable![31]
It seems I've been in quite some danger.
So, never trust a flower arranger!"

---

[28] opted for – chose
[29] accelerate – start moving faster
[30] undeniable – no doubt about it
[31] unreliable – something you can't trust

Jack and the Beanstalk

3.   Jack and the Beanstalk

A young boy, Jack, lived with his mum.
Sadly, mother's brain was numb.
Old and permanently sour,[32]
Her brains were made of cauliflower.

The Beanstalk family had been rich,
But a neighbour, little snitch,[33]
Revealed just where the gold was hidden.
And so, one Sunday night, unbidden[34],

Came a giant down the road
And nicked[35] the lot, the greedy toad!
The cart was full, there was no more,
The Beanstalks now were awfully poor!

One night, young Jack dreamed something strange,
Which made him think, "Things have to change!"
A wise old fairy, voice like honey,
Told him where to get the money.

After this nocturnal[36] flashback
He thought, "We need to get our cash back!"
He googled "giant", "steal" and "loot",[37]
Pressed "enter", then he got the route.

---

[32] sour – (here) bad-tempered
[33] snitch – person who gives away secrets, tells people things he shouldn't
[34] unbidden – secretly
[35] nick – steal
[36] nocturnal – something which happens at night
[37] loot – things which have been stolen

He texted friends to give assistance
And overcome the giant's resistance.
They came at once, all in good cheer,[38]
The influence of Jack's free beer.

A road sign told them, clear as day,
"The giant's castle? Climb this way!
You'd better have a long-ish rope,
If not, you haven't got a hope!"

"Hah! A climb of ninety metres
Up a cliff sure won't defeat us!"
But his friends said, out of breath,
"We're not too keen on certain death!"

Unsure about a plan of action,
They waited for young Jack's reaction.
He thought about it, then he said,
"Let's go down the pub instead."

Seated in the pub with beer,
All were happy, of good cheer.
But, of course, it couldn't last,
For they soon heard this vocal blast.[39]

"Hello Jack, of beanstalk fame,
Everybody knows your name!
But mine, of course, nobody knows,
Three guesses, just be on your toes!"

---

[38] in good cheer – very happy
[39] vocal blast – (here) loud voice

"For God's sake, Rumpy, little toad!
Just shut your trap[40] and hit the road.
All of us know who you are,
So, stamp your feet and fetch your car!"

The next day, Monday, market day,
At sunrise, Jack was on his way.
They had to eat, wondered how,
Decided they must sell the cow.

A decision that was hard to make,
But both were sick of vegan steak.
Mum said, "We need the money, hurry!
I need to stuff myself with curry!"

Round the corner Jack stood still,
Saw a strange man by the mill.
He thought, "The market's miles away,
I'll see what he has got to say."

"That mangy[41] cow just can't be real,
If you want, I'll do a deal.
The cow is mine, and that means
You can keep these magic beans!

Take them home and give them mum,
It's well known that she's pretty dumb.
She won't know what the things are for,
But see she chucks[42] them out the door!"

---

[40] Shut your trap! – Shut your mouth!
[41] mangy – in poor condition
[42] chuck – throw

It happened thus and so, next morning,
Jack got up as day was dawning.
Peeking[43] out the front, he saw
A beanstalk never seen before.

A sign said, "If you want your gold,
This way up, lo and behold[44]!
Up you go, and mind, no stopping,
'Cause the giant's gone out shopping!"

Considering the task ahead,
Jack had a fag[45], and then he said,
"It must be me, 'cause mum won't go
Besides, her brains are made of dough.

Fighting giants is worse than death,
Because I soon get out of breath.
I start to get all anaerobic
Because, you know, I'm fee-fi-phobic.[46]

Golden goose and talking harp,
I'll get both if I look sharp.[47]
And if I really make a dash,
I'll also grab the bags of cash."

He climbed the stalk, but at the top,
He met the giant at the shop.
The giant stopped and then he stared,
"It's my birthday!" he declared.

---

[43] peek – have quick look (usually from behind the curtain)
[44] lo and behold – "Look at this" (usually said when presenting sth.
   spectacular
[45] fag – BrE cigarette
[46] "Fee fi fo fum" is what the giant says in the traditional fairy tale. "Fee-fi-
   phobic" means "scared of giants who say this".
[47] look sharp – if I am quick

"The tales imply I'm pretty dumb
For saying fee - fi - fo and fum!
They say that I just scream and shout.
From now on I'll just leave it out!"

There was in fact no need to talk,
He chased poor Jack right down the stalk.
The goose and harp, if truth be told,
Were on the stalk too, counting gold.

Jack exclaimed, "I need help fast!"
His luck was in, for walking past,
He saw a travelling sales gorilla,
Who had some instant beanstalk killer.

He grabbed a can and saying "Ook,"
Read the brief instruction book,
He dashed back to the stalk, took aim,
But started, as he heard his name.

"Jack Beanstalk! You come here, this minute!
That's instant beanstalk killer, innit?
Smells much worse than Polyfilla,[48]
It's all the fault of that gorilla!

Chuck it out! It's not organic.
The sight of it just makes me panic!
You spray that stuff here in our garden,
You'll kill the plants, there'll be no pardon!"

Jack said, "Mum, you silly chump!
You've just really made me jump!
I didn't get a direct hit,
But missed the stalk with most of it!"

---

[48] Polyfilla – material used for filling cracks in walls

Instead of killing it completely,
The stalk collapsed, both slow and neatly.
And thanks to Jack's unsteady hand,
The giant floated down to land.

The giant said, "I've got you now!
You'll rue the day you sold that cow!"
And shouting loud, "You'll soon be dead!"
He chased them round the garden shed.

In the house, upstairs and down,
Past the kitchen, round and round.
Jack shouted out, "Quick! In the bedroom,
We'll profit from the lack of headroom!"[49]

A bad mistake, they stopped to stare.
The giant was already there!
He licked his lips and said, "Hooray!
Breakfast time in bed today!"

Pros and cons were quickly weighed.
Jack's mum said, a bit afraid,
(The giant towered high above her)
"It's "Curtains Weekly[50]", we're front cover!"

A hoover[51] flew right o'er the bed,
And hit the giant on the head.
There came a voice from out of sight,
(From behind the curtain, on the right.)

---

[49] lack of headroom – the ceiling is low
[50] „It's curtains" – "It's the end for us!" "Curtains Weekly" – an imaginary magazine dealing with people in difficult situations. Jack and his mum are in such a difficult situation that they are on the front cover of this magazine.
[51] hoover – vacuum cleaner

"No need to ask whence[52] comes the hoover.
It's me, the famous giant remover!
Old Rumpy said you were in trouble,
So, I came here on the double."[53]

An egg came wobbling into view.
Jack wiped his brow and murmured, "phew!
Hello Humpty, that's the way!
Once again, you've saved the day!"

"Well, things were looking pretty sticky.
Giants can be pretty tricky.
When choosing weapons to project,[54]
A hoover has the best effect.

And by the way, I think you'll see
(But not entirely thanks to me)
That when the beanstalk gently fell,
Your former riches fell as well!"

[52] whence – from where
[53] on the double – very quickly
[54] project – throw

Cindy and the Prince

4. Cindy and the Prince

And now a tale whose central theme
Revolves around a young girl's dream
To make her lifelong dream come true,
Using nothing but a shoe.

Young Cinderella was no fool.
She thought the dashing[55] prince was cool.
She said, "I want to be with him,
It doesn't matter if he's dim[56]!"

Well aware of the traditions,
She knew, of course, there'd be conditions.
There was, of course, the palace ball,
She'd go disguised[57], and then she'd fall.

Tradition said she'd leave a shoe,
So the prince knew what to do.
He would find her, she'd be queen,
(With lots of luck, by Halloween).

She knew it wouldn't be so easy,
The thought alone just made her queasy.[58]
The whole thing never could be painless -
The Prince was absolutely brainless.

---

[55] dashing – good-looking
[56] dim – not very clever
[57] disguised – wearing different clothes so nobody will recognise you
[58] queasy – feeling ill

Cindy's mum thought "What to do?
The prince has got a low IQ.
In fact, as far as I recall,[59]
He hasn't an IQ at all."

 "You'll have to leave more shoes behind
For the dozy prince to find.
It's not enough just on the stair,
You'll have to leave them everywhere!

You'll need at least a dozen shoes,
He's going to need a lot of clues.
Above, below, in front, behind him,
Everywhere, just to remind him."

Cindy said, "Well, night is falling.
Our preparations are appalling[60].
Tradition here is most precise,
We need some lizards, rats and mice."

"Well," said mum, "That might be hard.
We had a chat down in the yard.
The animals are quite frustrating,
Don't feel like cooperating.

The rats, they could be problematic.
They're all on strike up in the attic.
They've handed in a protest letter,
Saying mice are treated better.

---

[59] recall - remember
[60] appalling - terrible

The lizards too, are overrated.[61]
Most of them have hibernated.[62]
The one that's left, despite his slowness,
Wants a nighttime working bonus.

On top of that, the farmyard cat
Devotes his days to getting fat.
In fact, the whole damn farm's on strike.
You might as well just use the bike!"

"The bike?" She couldn't believe her ears.
"That's not been used for fifty years!
That rusty thing will make me late.
Won't even make it past the gate!"

Said Cinderella's fairy mum,
"The situation's pretty dumb.
But don't worry, it's not tragic,
I can do a bit of magic."

She waved her wand, a flash of light,
And there before them, shining bright,
(Cindy'd never seen the like)[63],
A brand-new, modern racing bike.

"How cool is that!" young Cindy cried.
"Now don't forget!" her mum replied,
"Carbon frame and thirty gears,
But at twelve it disappears!"

---

[61] overrated – not as good as people think
[62] hibernate – go to sleep for the winter
[63] the like – anything similar, anything like it

Her list of things to do, meanwhile,
Almost filled a ten-page file.
To use her time as a commuter[64],
She had an onboard bike computer.

Avoiding all the rush hour traps,
She planned her route on Google maps.
"And then, before I travel there,
I really have to wash my hair!"

Next, a suitable disguise,
So he gets a big surprise.
The last thing I must do is choose
A rucksack for these extra shoes!"

But all this work made Cindy late –
She set off for the palace gate.
Once there, she parked and locked her bike.
Went in, looking businesslike.

Now and then she tried to eat,
But had no time, rushed off her feet,
In between bites of spaghetti,
Scattered shoes round like confetti.

Cindy thought, "I need a chance
To grab the prince and have a dance.
I'll just have time to say hello,
Then grab the bike and off I'll go."

The dashing Prince was bored to tears,
The minutes simply seemed like years,
When, propping up the royal bar,
He spied young Cindy from afar.

---

[64] commuter – a person who travels to and from work regularly

The prince thought, "Here's a girl I like!"
He asked her all about the bike.
Excited by the carbon frame,
He quite forgot to ask her name.

At breakfast, drinking pots of tea,
The prince thought, "Oh God, silly me!
Mum will never be forgiving.
I have to find out where she's living!"

Everywhere, on stairs, in loos,
He kept on finding Cindy's shoes.
Thought, at this discovery,
She must be leaving hints[65] for me!

Putting on his royal cape,
He set off down the fire escape.
By the time he'd reached the floor,
He'd even found a couple more.

"That's it!" he murmured, sitting down.
Tomorrow morn I'm off to town.
I'll check on every girl I meet
To see if they've got thirty feet.

Through the village, the next day,
People came to shout hooray.
Carefully placed at intersections[66]
To give the prince the right directions.

The prince cried, "Wolf! You're here in town!
Come to blow some houses down?"
What's on your T-shirt? "Watch this space!
Here's the route to Cindy's place?"

---

[65] hints – clues
[66] intersections – crossroads

A travelling salesman in a cap
Sold the king a simple map.
An arrow pointed down the road,
Straight to Cindy's farm abode.

And when the prince once went astray,[67]
They helped him back upon his way.
The villagers, most helpful folk,
Made shoe-like signals out of smoke.

Arriving at the farm quite late,
The prince met Cindy at the gate.
But! Before he could sit down beside her,
He shouted, "Look! A massive spider!

Its legs are long and very hairy!
Not for me, it's just too scary!
Call the butler! Call the chauffeur!
I'll just hide behind the sofa."

Behind the sofa he did choose
He found another pile of shoes.
He thought, "Ah, Cindy's got a sister!
She's probably out, I must have missed her."

An egg arrived and said, "Good morning!"
Couldn't stop himself from yawning.
Humpty Dumpty was the name
(He of bug-removing fame).

"The prince," he said, "is total crap!
Quite a nervous sort of chap.
But let me just remove my hat,
I'll sit on it and squash it flat."

---

[67] went astray – got lost

47

But Humpty didn't do a lot,
The spider vanished like a shot.
Humpty's widespread reputation
Meant instant spider abdication[68].

Humpty was then heard to say,
"The problem's solved, I'm on my way!"
But once outside these words he spoke,
"I'm done. Just look! My car is broke!"

He said, "Whatever should I do?
I have to deal with quite a queue!"
But then a voice, "No need to panic!
I'm a part time car mechanic!

No need for an instruction book.
I, the prince, will have a look!
Once I've found out just what's wrong,
I'll have it fixed before too long."

His expert eye soon found the cause.
This earned him thunderous applause.
The prince's engineering cunning[69]
Soon got old Humpty's engine running.

The villagers all cheered outside.
Cinderella beamed with pride.
Humpty's car was on its way, and
T'was the prince who'd saved the day!

---

[68] abdication – normally describes when a king or queen decides not to reign
anymore. Here it describes the spider leaving the house very quickly
[69] cunning – skill

The Three Little Pigs

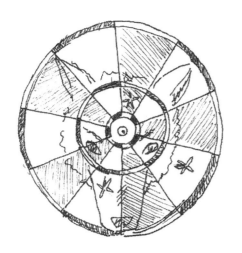

5.   The Three Little Pigs

Mummy pig was in a mood.
She was sick of cooking food.
Also tired of constant cleaning,
She often thought "It's so demeaning![70]

No one ever thinks of me,
All I hear is, "What's for tea?"
She said, "The kids are kids no more!
The youngest one is 34!"

Pigs one and two were downright[71] lazy,
The thought of work just drove them crazy.
They stuffed themselves with strawberry tarts
And spent their evenings playing darts.

Both of them, though fit and able,
Scarcely[72] left the dining table.
From noon till late they filled their belly,
And also watched the darts on telly.

Pig three never stayed up late, though
He, too, was a couch potato.
Watched History Channel every week,
A mediaeval castle freak.

One day, while mum was cleaning shoes,
She heard an item on the news.
A pig psychology professor,
Whose words of wisdom did impress her.

---

[70] it's so demeaning – nobody respects the work I do
[71] downright – completely
[72] scarcely - hardly

"Over thirty is an age,
Where pigs can earn a living wage.
They should live at home no more -
Show the lazy things the door!"

"Yes!" came her triumphant shout.
"It's time all three of them were out!"
And before they knew it, that same day,
Three little pigs were on their way.

Pig one cried, out in the yard,
"Building houses can't be hard!"
"Doesn't really need much thought!"
Was piggy number two's retort.[73]

Meanwhile on the edge of town,
The wolf considered, with a frown,
His unsuccessful hunting past,
And thought, "I need some food, and fast!"

He sat down, carefully thought it through,
Then cried, "I know just what to do!
I'll have a wander into town,
And try and blow some houses down.

Quietly I'll nose about
And check the piggies' houses out.
And once I've got inside all three,
The pigs will soon be inside me!"

Pig one, although against the law,
Had nicked[74] a neighbour's pile of straw.
Not really knowing how or why,
He piled it up into the sky.

"Well, that's that!" he cried with glee.[75]
"That's my building done for me!
My building work is purest art.
But now it's time for strawberry tart!"

---

[73] retort – answer
[74] nicked – stolen
[75] glee – happiness

But for the tart he had to wait,
'Cause when they reached the garden gate,
The happiness they'd felt that day
Soon began to fade away.[76]

Appearing like a Cheshire cat,[77]
An old man in a pointy hat,
A face just like a rubbish bin,
Shouted with an evil grin,

"Ok, piggies, here's the game.
Bet you'll never guess my name.
Guesses you get up to three,
Then your house belongs to me!"

Pig one said, "We don't need your test.
Cork it[78], Rumpy, you're a pest!
What your name is, we all know.
Stamp your foot and off you go!"

Pig two had found a pile of wood.
He could build, or, thought he could.
He cried, "You need to use your head!"
Then built a wobbly garden shed.

It looked like if you closed the door
Too hard, then it would stand no more.
"No wolf will never bother me,"
He said and went to watch TV.

---

[76] fade away – disappear slowly
[77] Cheshire cat – character from the children's story "Alice in
   Wonderland" – a cat that could just appear and disappear.
[78] Cork it! – if you put a cork in a bottle of wine you close it. Here it
   means simply "shut up!"

The third pig was a building master.
Knew all about cement and plaster.
Not a fan of straw or sticks,
He'd ordered thirty tons of bricks.

At 4 o'clock, their work complete,
All three pigs put up their feet.
Then through the window pig one saw
A wolf approach his house of straw.

The wolf came closer, dropped his jaw.
He'd never seen a house of straw.
He cried, "I thought it was a rumour,
This pig has got a sense of humour!"

The wolf said, "Dear me, it's hilarious![79]
I've never seen one so precarious.[80]
Will you take a look at that?
I could sneeze and knock it flat!

It could, in fact, be easier still,
I know what would fit the bill[81]!
If I lean against the door,
The house will tumble to the floor!"

But before the wolf could start,
He felt the impact of a dart.
He shouted, "Hey, what's that there?
Using darts is just not fair!"

---

[79] hilarious – very funny
[80] precarious – (here) likely to fall down any minute
[81] fit the bill – if sth fits the bill, it is perfect

Then another, then lots more,
The wolf retreated from the door.
Feeling anything but fine,
And looking like a porcupine[82].

Puffing hard (and also blowing),
But didn't watch where he was going!
He stubbed his toes, banged his knee,
And hit his head against a tree.

A little further down the road
He saw the second pig's abode.[83]
He thought, "The last was close to falling.
But this one here is just appalling[84]!

The whole thing looks a touch unsteady,
It's almost falling down already.
As building goes, he's quite a loser.
Plays too much darts down at the boozer."[85]

The wolf considered with a frown,
"It won't take long to blow it down."
But as the Wolf was trying to start,
He felt another pointy dart.

He yelped and shouted,"Not again!
Dart-playing piggies are a pain!"
Abandoning his dinner goal,
He turned and fell into a hole.

---

[82] porcupine – animal with long spines, like a hedgehog, but bigger.
[83] abode – place where someone lives
[84] appalling – terrible
[85] boozer – pub

Some days later, rather lame,
He carried on his hunting game.
He thought, "Today at least it's clear.
There'll be no flying darts to fear!"

He made his journey through the wood
To where the piggy's house now stood.
Turned a corner, rubbed his eyes,
Exclaimed quite loudly in surprise.

In front of him there stood a sort
Of mediaeval royal fort.
Pig three had been enthusiastic,
Planned a building quite fantastic.

Complete with drawbridge[86] and a moat[87]
So wide that you would need a boat,
A sign said, "Wolves can blow all day,
They'll never blow this one away!"

The pig stood on the ramparts[88], smirking,
Above just where the wolf was lurking.[89]
Called down, "So, wolf, what's the plan?
Come and get me if you can!"

Wolf stopped and stared as if in pain.
He said, "I'll have to think again.
What with castles, moats and darts,
I'll have to move to foreign parts."

---

[86] drawbridge – a bridge that can be pulled up, leading into a castle
[87] moat – a ditch full of water surrounding a castle
[88] ramparts – the high outer walls of a castle
[89] lurk – wait in hiding

So, the moral of this tale
Is that you will never fail,
And that it's never, ever wrong
To watch the telly all day long!

Wolves can blow
all day,
they'll never blow
this one away!

The Frog Prince

6.   The Frog Prince

In a castle far away
A princess lived, who every day,
Went down to the local park,
Where she played from dawn till dark.

She usually, a royal perk,[90]
Got someone else to do her work.
And so, she had a servant gang
Who she normally would harangue[91]

To gather all the royal toys
And, avoiding any noise,
Take them out for her to play,
And wait on her throughout the day.

The staff could simply not abide her
Couldn't stand to be beside her.
As soon as she began to play,
They did their best to slip away.

The chauffeur went to mend the car,
The gardener slipped off to the bar.
The butler found a pond to dredge,[92]
Then had a smoke behind the hedge.

Whenever she ran out of steam[93],
She'd lie down and start to dream.
But no dreams of a golden ball!
What she wanted most of all,

---

[90] perk – privilege
[91] harangue – talk loudly at
[92] dredge a lake – remove sand from the bottom
[93] run out of steam – have no energy left

Which would be her pride and joy,
Her super-favourite royal toy,
The thing she really wished to own,
A lilac royal mobile phone!

She mentioned this to dad one day
Hoping she would get her way.
"I saw an advert in the town,
The same place where we rent the crown!

'This is something you must own,
Your personal royal mobile phone!
Text and surf until you drop!'
It says so in the village shop!"

Surprise, surprise, a fortnight later
There came to her a royal waiter.
In his hand a kitchen tray,
And something new, with which to play.

Her toys she played with less and less,
Learned to send an SMS.
Used Google, YouTube and WhatsApp,
Filled her brain with online crap.

She played with it from dawn till late.
But one day, trying to concentrate,
Startled[94] by a nearby bell,
She dropped her mobile down the well.

The princess shouted loud, "Oh hell!
I've gone and dropped it down the well!
I'll have to jump down after it,
My dad, the king, will have a fit!"[95]

---

[94] startled – suddenly shocked
[95] have a fit – be very angry

65

At this point a young-ish frog,
Sitting on a nearby log[96],
Said, "Princess, I can help you there,
And stop the king from going spare![97]

To help our good king's youngest daughter,
I'll gladly jump into the water.
Swim down where the water's black
And you will have your mobile back!

But what I'd like," the frog implored,[98]
"Is in return a small reward.
Something you can do for me,
Invite me home with you for tea."

---

[96] log – large piece of wood
[97] go spare – cf ([67] -get very angry
[98] implore – beg

"It's a deal!" she said, and thought,
"No worries, it will come to naught![99]
A promise that's not hard to give
Frogs have memories like a sieve!"

When all were having tea next day,
The princess heard, to her dismay,
A sound that she had heard before -
A froggy voice outside the door.

"Hello princess this is me!
Your froggy friend, I've come to tea!
You said that tea is served at four.
I'm starving, so unlock the door!"

The king was known for being fair,
And asked the princess, "Who? What? Where?"
She replied, "He helped poor me,
So I invited him to tea!"

Ignoring the princess's frown,
The king said, "Please, come in, sit down!
Next to me, a comfy seat,
Now tell us what you'd like to eat!"

The frog hopped in and took the chair.
Avoiding the princess's glare.
Thought about it for a while,
Answered with a froggy smile,

"What I like to eat the most
Is beetle pie or flies on toast.
When it's warm you just can't beat it
Princess, you should try to eat it!"

---

[99] naught – nothing

This plunged[100] her into deep despair.
She stamped and cried and pulled her hair.
She shouted, "This is just not on[101]!
Talk to him and say, "Begone![102]"

His skin looks like it's started rusting,
His table manners are disgusting!
No-one knows just where he's been,
Look at him, the thing's bright green!

I can't sit there and eat pork pies
When he's beside me, eating flies!
Dad, don't let him spoil the day.
Tell the thing to go away!"

The king, however, made it clear.
"Mr. Frog will stay right here,
And since he saved the royal phone,
Can have a seat all of his own."

But before he managed to say more
There was a knock upon the door.
It opened slowly with a creak,
And through it came a circus freak.

Trying hard to be all hearty[103],
The death of every royal party,
He bowed down low before the king
And tunelessly began to sing...

---

[100] plunged her into despair – made her despair
[101] that's not on! – we can't allow that!
[102] Begone! – Go away!
[103] hearty – cheerful

"Good evening all! Your Majesty!
May I point out courteously[104],
Our traditional guessing game
To find out just what is my name?"

All present thought, "Oh, not that git[105]!"
But Kingy made the best of it.
Determined not to spoil the meal,
A massive groan he did conceal.

"Evening, Rumpy, come right in!
Grab your usual pint of gin.
Find a chair, or stool, or log
And sit you down next to the frog."

The frog meanwhile had drunk right up
His gin out of his three-pint cup.
Halfway through his third dessert,
He lay there totally inert.[106]

Some while later up he spoke
And said, "These armchairs are a joke!
What I need to rest my head
Is a comfy royal bed!"

The princess shouted "What? No way!
In my bed till break of day?
Someone grab that cheeky feller[107]
Lock him up down in the cellar!"

---

[104] courteously - politely
[105] git – stupid person, idiot
[106] inert – without moving
[107] feller (fellow) – person

The king then cleared his throat once more,
Said, "Ok, listen! Here's the score!
This frog deserves a good night's rest,
A comfy room, one of the best.

A room with a fantastic view,
So, he'll be sharing yours with you.
He looks a bit the worse for wear,[108]
You'll have to carry him up the stair."

The poor princess could take no more,
She bounced him on the bedroom floor,
Like a rubber tennis ball,
Then chucked him hard against the wall.

"Well, that should be the end of that!"
She waited for a massive splat[109].
But no splat came to make her wince[110],
Instead there stood a handsome prince!

"Now that's a turn-up for the books!"
She said, and thought, "fantastic looks!
Up I had a frog to carry,
Down I'll take a prince to marry!"

She cried, "I wasn't expecting that!
Here stands a prince and not a splat.
Looks like you have been bewitched,
But now you're not, so let's get hitched![111]"

---

[108] looks the worse for wear – not in very good condition
[109] splat – the sound made by a wet object hitting sth. hard
[110] wince – to show, by an expression on your face, that you are
  embarrassed or feel pain.
[111] get hitched – (colloquial) get married

The prince said, "Great!" Then, "Right away!"
But added, in a serious way,
"From now on please be kind to frogs
Who talk to you and sit on logs!"

The princess cried, "Consider it done!
Now let's get down and join the fun!"
They ate and drank, enjoyed the band,
And soon the wedding date was planned.

So once more a happy ending.
A royal wedding now impending!
You want to hear a wedding bell?
Then chuck your mobile down the well!

The Three Other Bears

7.   The Three Other Bears

Many, many years ago,
In a land that we don't know,
There lived a family of bears,
Who suffered disapproving stares.

Related to, but not the same,
As the bears of porridge fame,
They knew one thing with certitude[112],
They had no time for healthy food.

"Cooking leads to poor nutrition,"
Said bear one without contrition.[113]
"But steak is always best done well,
And I prefer it burned to hell."

Listening in, bear number two,
Adding sausage to his stew,
Said, "I agree with you, old bear.
I've no time for healthy fare!"[114]

Bear three, who finished every dish,
Smoked cigars, drank like a fish.
On top of all the alcohol,
He binged out[115] on cholesterol.

The three of them, to great surprise,
When not consuming piles of fries,
Were busy in the private sector,
Each one as a food inspector.

---

[112] with certitude – for sure
[113] without contrition – with no regrets
[114] fare – food
[115] binge out – eat way too much

Checking restaurants, never late,
They rarely failed to clean the plate.
They even all, when testing fries,
Complained about the portion size.

But, truth be told, the bears were stingy,[116]
Their cave was dark and cold and dingy.[117]
Spurning[118] porridge, seeking trout,
At breakfast time they all dined out.

Although demanding quality,
They made sure that they ate for free.
Round the country they would roam[119],
To find a house with no-one home.

Avoiding things remotely healthy,
They chose the houses of the wealthy.
They'd zoom off in their motor car
And feast on trout and caviar.

Unlike their cousins, picky[120] lot,
These bears ate both: cold and hot.
Being a pretty lazy bunch,
They'd find a bed and sleep till lunch.

The problem was, such gourmet bears
Had massive problems climbing stairs.
Faced with such an overload,
Most stairs would instantly implode.

---

[116] stingy – mean
[117] dingy – dark, boring
[118] spurn – ignore something because it's not good enough
[119] roam - travel
[120] picky – fussy, choosy

One morning, having eaten grouse[121]
In a chosen breakfast house
So clean that it felt almost creepy,
They started feeling rather sleepy.

But then, an irritating voice!
They had to listen, had no choice!
Towering over our three bears
From the top of broken stairs…

"Hello bears, you greedy lot
Was the porridge cold or hot?
By the way, a funny game
Would be to try and guess my name!

A thing no-one has ever done!
Guess my name? It can't be done!
For decades everyone has tried,
The information's classified!

The bears looked up, and sighed, and then
They said, "Oh God, it's him again!
He's here again! He never fails.
He gets in all the fairy tales!"

"Hello Rumpy, just in time.
This caviare is quite sublime!
Just stamp your foot upon the floor,
And disappear and get some more!"

Rumpy cried "Oh damn and blast!
My anonymity is past!"
And added, with a heartfelt groan,
"I'll have to stop, my name is known!"

---

[121] grouse – wild bird (German – Moorhuhn)

This time, at last he got it right.
Disappeared into the night.
Stamped his foot upon the floor,
Vanished and was seen no more!

This eating problem was a curse.
The bear police just made it worse.
The only started work at one,
By then the greedy bears were gone!

Humpty couldn't come that day.
He'd gone away on holiday.
Two whole weeks in the Bahamas,
Spent the day in his pyjamas.

The bears all had a brilliant time,
Heartily enjoyed their crime,
Consuming, if I'm not mistaken,
Fantastic quantities of bacon.

They might have carried on forever,
Stealing breakfast food, however,
One day, they had to stop and stare.
They met a girl with golden hair.

Having breakfasted one day
In the usual greedy way,
They paused and said, "This house is funny!
It's totally devoid of [122]honey!"

"That's correct!" A voice declared.
The bears looked up the stairs and stared.
And heard, by way of explanation,
"I don't support bee exploitation[123]!

---

[122] devoid of – completely without
[123] exploitation – taking advantage of sth./sb.

I fail to see why a bee
Should make its honey just for me.
Outside the clubs on Friday nights
I campaign for apian[124] rights."

The bears just listened, all in awe[125]
They'd never heard the word before.
Nor ever read it, even seen!
What on earth did "apian" mean?

Bear one murmured, "Huh? Why traipse[126]
Around the nightclubs helping apes?"
Bear two, "It's double Dutch to me,
We'll have to ask bear number three."

---

[124] apian – connected with bees
[125] in awe – amazed
[126] traipse – walk around slowly, without any real direction

Bear three explained the mystery
(He'd studied etymology)
"It's bees!" he said, then, "Don't be funny,
That's the reason there's no honey!"

Bear number one exclaimed, "Whatever!
To me it all sounds really clever!
Listen up to what she says.
I think we need to change our ways!"

He shouted without hesitation,
"I want to try out meditation!"
He said, "I'm going to find out more
Where's the esoteric store?

Even if it costs a bomb,
I'm going to spend my life with Om!"
And added, "You can stuff your bees!
I'll spend my mornings hugging trees!"

Bear two, "I'm good with words, I ought ter[127]
Make a fortune selling water.
Become a doctor, curing ills
With homeopathic sugar pills."

Bear three was getting all excited.
Shouted loud "We'll all get knighted![128]"
Goldie said, "That's not the way!
Listen here to what I say!

Have you forgotten you are bears?
You shouldn't go round breaking stairs!
Bears are clever, bears are strong.
Bears help others all day long"

---

[127] "ought ter" – ought to
[128] get knighted – be given the title of "Sir" by the Queen

And from that day the bears reformed.
The population's hearts were warmed.
They started mending people's stairs,
Providing old-age wolves with chairs.

They cleaned an aging dog's abode,
Helped young hedgehogs cross the road,
Knitted socks to warm cold feet,
And helped the poor to make ends meet.[129]

---

[129] make ends meet – have enough money to live on

They even started giving money
To make sure homeless bears had honey.
Though, to be fair I have to say,
Young Goldie looked the other way.

Young Goldie was quite satisfied.
People praised her far and wide.
From his Bahaman island yard,
Even Humpty sent a card.

And so you'll find up to this day,
Thanks to Goldie, animals may
Live safely, have a happy time,
And breakfast theft is not a crime.

Hansel and Gretel

8.   Hansel and Gretel

Many many years ago,
In a tiny bungalow,
A woman lived, down by the ditch[130],
Thought by some to be a witch.

For most there was no doubt, although,
Some people asked, "But how d'you know?"
They said, "There are no witches here?"
But for most t'was pretty clear.

Of course, she really looked the part,
Struck terror into every heart.
Wore the usual pointy hat,
Had the standard witch's cat.

A massive wart upon her nose,
Magic wands, yes lots of those.
Hissed and cackled[131] all the night,
Yes, she was a witch alright!

But one small thing, it must be said,
There was no trace of gingerbread.
This she had at once rejected,
Though she knew it was expected.

"You would never see me dead
In a house of gingerbread!
A house like that just isn't cool.
To live there, you must be a fool!

---

[130] ditch – long, narrow hole in the ground
[131] cackle – the evil laughing sound made by a witch

The birds, they love it, that's the curse.
They eat it, and to make it worse,
They steal what's left and use the rest
To build a ginger-flavoured nest.

You come home, day's work completed,
Find that half the door's been eated!
Two weeks later, they don't care.
You're living in the open air!

Mine just looks like gingerbread,
Authentic though! It's often said,
An edible[132] house is overrated,[133]
Mine can simply be inflated!"

Nobody there was ever seen,
Till, quite by chance, one Hallowe'en,
Through the woods there came one day,
A boy and girl who'd lost their way.

Round and round the local park,
Through the woods from dawn till dark,
Their dad had done his best to lose them,
Here and there, just to confuse them.

A word of explanation here:
Dad loved his kids, that much was clear,
But being more than stony broke,[134]
He hoped they'd find a kindly bloke[135]

---

[132] edible – can be eaten
[133] overrated – not as good as people think
[134] stony broke – having no money at all
[135] bloke – man

With a family in the city,
Who'd find them both and then take pity.
He'd take them home and with his wife
They'd give the kids a better life.

And so, let the two kids play,
Then quietly he slipped away.
The two of them were quite surprised,
When they suddenly realised

That dad was gone, they were alone!
They both took out their mobile phone.
Before ten minutes could elapse,[136]
They'd found the route on Google Maps.

"We must get back and find our dad,
But the fog is really bad.
We'd have to be completely loopy[137]
To try it now, it's much too soupy."[138]

"A wobbly[139] little house!" Hans said,
"Looks like mouldy[140] gingerbread.
The state of it is pretty drastic,
Seems to have been made of plastic!

We'll go and ask there, never fear!
There's prob'ly only some old dear.
The house looks warm enough alright.
Maybe we can stay the night?

---

[136] elapse – go past
[137] loopy – mad
[138] soupy – my thanks to Nils, Clara and Elli from Australia for giving me this word ☺
[139] wobbly – unsteady
[140] mouldy – when green and blue fungus grows on bread which is old and damp

And, you never know, we might
Even get to scrounge[141] a bite.
We'll maybe even get to grips
With burgers, peas and piles of chips!"

Just a couple of minutes more
And they were knocking at the door.
But, being plastic, t'was a shock,
To merely[142] hear a squeaky knock.

Standing on a bouncy floor,
Next to an inflated door,
Gretel said, "It's as I feared.
This is getting really weird!"

---

[141] scrounge – beg
[142] merely – only

Even though it just looks sleepy,
I think that it's much too creepy.
Then they saw a pointy hat,
Magic wand and witch's cat!

"Welcome children! Nice to eat you!
Sorry! I meant nice to **meet** you!
You'll be wanting information,
Overnight accommodation!

You must be dying on your feet!
You prob'ly want some things to eat.
Food I have both cold and hot,
Let me tell you what we've got!

A massive choice of things to eat,
The problem is, I'm short of meat.
Piles of carrots, spuds[143] and leeks,
But no butcher here for weeks!

But now it matters not one whit[144] –
You two have put an end to it.
I've 'a place that you'll be lovin'
You'll both be sleeping in the oven!"

Young Hans declared, "That wasn't planned!
"Restaurants like this are banned!
We need some disobedience[145]!
If not, then we're ingredients!"

---

[143] spuds – (colloquial) - potatoes
[144] it matters not one whit – it doesn't matter at all
[145] disobedience – not following orders

A hooting[146] sound, an egg-shaped car,
Help approaching from afar!
And looking tough and very mean,
Humpty roared upon the scene.

"Sometimes sooner, sometimes later,
I'm the famous house deflater!
We've hurried here from foreign parts,
Piggies, please unpack your darts!"

---

[146] hoot – the sound of a car horn

Behind him piggies one and two
Knew exactly what to do!
A hail of darts[147] across the ground,
Followed by a hissing sound.

The witch cried, "That's the end for me!
Humpty's a calamity[148]!"
And sensing her impending[149] doom,
She kick-started her ancient broom.

Inside they found, it must be told,
The usual hidden hoard of gold.
The kids no longer had to roam,
But could afford to live at home.

Before the piggies did depart,
They feasted all on strawberry tart,
And explained (while adding cream)
How they joined old Humpty's team.

---

[147] a hail of darts – a lot of darts flying through the air at the same time
[148] calamity – disaster
[149] impending – coming closer

9.   About the author

Neil Stainthorpe is a native English speaker, English teacher and teacher trainer with over 33 years experience at the Pädagogische Hochschule der Diözese Linz (formerly Pädagogische Akademie).

He grew up in England in the West Midlands, then studied Modern Foreign Languages at the University of Leeds, before training to be an English teacher.
Additionally, he taught for many years at primary level, where he was able to combine guitar playing, singing and playing games, and managed to get away with calling it work. ☺

contact: neil.stainthorpe@ph-linz.at

10.   About the illustrator

Cornelia Kriechbaumer has been fond of art since her early childhood and uses drawings and paintings to express herself.

She decided to combine art, design and technology by studying architecture at the Kunstuniversität in Linz, where she completed her degree in 2019.

She lives in Linz and is currently working in the field of architecture, architecture education, illustration and design.

11. By the same author

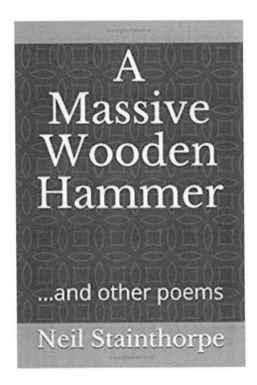

Have you ever...

thought about using a hedgehog to solve your problems?
Or been the victim of a conspiracy?
Or wondered what fish think when they arrive at the fish market?

Then read on...!
(...and also find out about learner drivers, complaining neighbours, students, camping holidays and of course the significance of the massive wooden hammer!)

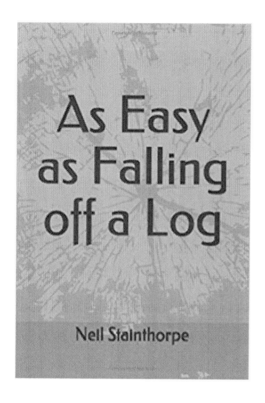

As Easy as Falling off a Log

Neil Stainthorpe

What do "skint," "wonky" and "gobsmacked" mean?
How does it feel to be "as sick as a parrot"?
Is it a good thing if you get on with someone "like a house on fire"?

300 everyday, colloquial English expressions in a fun quiz format with additional exercises.

All is not well on the farm!
What are the animals plotting? Does the farmer know?

Have you ever been on a holiday that wasn't quite what
you expected?

Do you really have a ball when you go to a ball?
Then read on...!

(...and also find out about New Year's resolutions,
modern art, incompetent pilots and much more!)

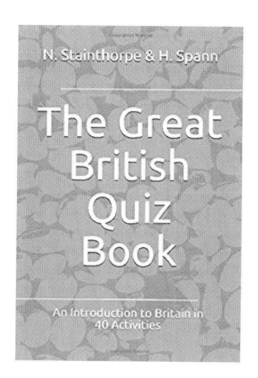

Britain is a fantastic place with fantastic people (yes, we know, there may be the odd exception ;-)
In this book we would like to share our common fascination for this wonderful place, its people, traditions and customs. It is a mixture of a critical look at the 'nature of Britishness' (whatever that is) in part 1, followed by a wide range of interesting and fun activities, quizzes and facts in part 2. This book is for students and teachers of English, anybody who loves doing quizzes, crosswords and other puzzles and who wants to find out more about Britain in a fun way.
(N. Stainthorpe & H. Spann)

Printed in Great Britain
by Amazon